Peppa's New Neighbours

Daddy Pig is working hard.
He is building a new house.

The new house looks
very small.
"Is it a house for elves
and fairies?" asks Peppa.
"No," chuckles Daddy Pig.
"This is just a model."

Daddy Pig shows
Peppa and George
a drawing of what
the real house
will look like.

"Something is missing!" says Peppa.

She draws a swing to go outside the house. "Perfect!" decides Daddy Pig.

Daddy Pig takes Peppa and
George to see the new house.

Brrrm!

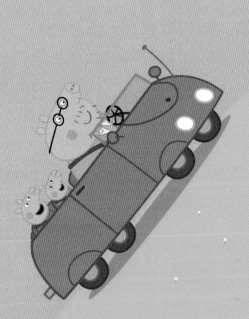

"Here we are!" he snorts.
"But Daddy," says Peppa,
"there's nothing here!"

Chug! Chug!

"That's because the building work hasn't started yet!" replies Daddy Pig.

Mr Bull is going to build the new house for Daddy Pig. "Can you build it exactly like this please?" says Daddy Pig.

"But bigger," adds Peppa.

Mr Bull shouts to his friends.
"Mr Pig wants a house!"
"Is it going to be built of straw?"
asks Mr Rhino.

"Or sticks?" asks Mr Labrador.
"Or bricks?" asks Mr Bull.

Daddy Pig wants the
new house to be made
out of bricks.

Mr Bull gets straight to work.
"Can we help?" wonders Peppa.
"You can lay the first brick," smiles Mr Bull.
Mr Bull tells George to put a blob of mortar
on the ground. Mortar is a special kind of mud
that sticks bricks together.

Each brick must be laid
straight and level.
It takes ages.
"Will you finish it
today?" asks Peppa.
"You can't build a house
in a day!" snorts Mr Bull.
"It will be finished ...
tomorrow."

The next morning, Peppa and George go
straight over to see the new house.
"It's finished!" snorts Peppa.
"It's almost finished!" says Daddy Pig.
"It just needs to be inspected."

Mr Rabbit is the building inspector.
He looks carefully at the new house.
"Very good," he decides, "but you forgot the swing!"

"Oh no we didn't!" shouts Mr Bull.

The house is all ready for the new neighbours
to move in. Mr Wolf and his family arrive.

Mr Wolf tries huffing and puffing, but the house doesn't fall down. It is very strong.
"What is the new house made of?" asks Mr Wolf.
"Bricks," replies Daddy Pig, "so don't even think about it."

Wendy Wolf likes the new swing.
"Can you push me?" asks Peppa.
"No," grins Wendy. "I'll huff and puff you instead!"

Hee!
Hee!

Flip Over Book

Two Books in One

Flip the book over for another fun story!

Flip Over Book

Two Books in One

Flip the book over for
another fun story!

Hooray!

"We win!" cries Danny. Captain Dog cheers.
"I'm not a sailor anymore," he says, "but I do love
boating on the lake!"

Everyone goes as fast as they can.
"I'm not sure I can pedal much
faster!" puffs Daddy Pig.
Captain Dog is lucky.
His boat has an engine.

"Let's see who can get back first,"
says Mummy Pig. "We'll have a race."

Ding!
Dong!

"Come in boats one, two
and three," she calls.
"Your time is up!"

"One, two and three?" says Peppa. "That's us!"

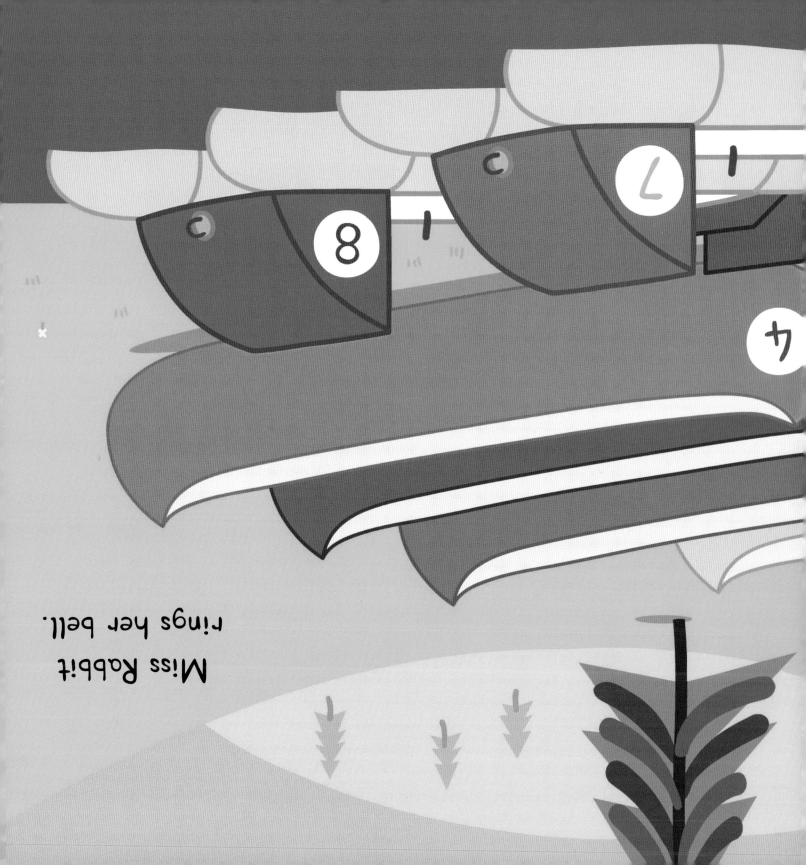

Miss Rabbit
rings her bell.

Everyone likes picnics!

It is time to stop for lunch.
Mummy Pig passes around the sandwiches.
"Here's some bread for you,
Mrs Duck," grins Peppa.
Mrs Duck likes picnics!

Quack!

Quack!

Poor Daddy Pig. Pedalling a pedalo is a lot harder than it looks.

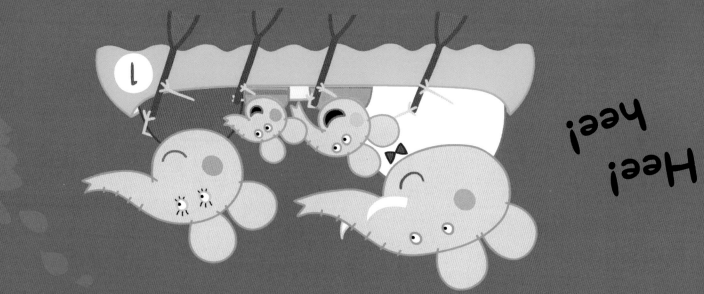

Hee! hee!

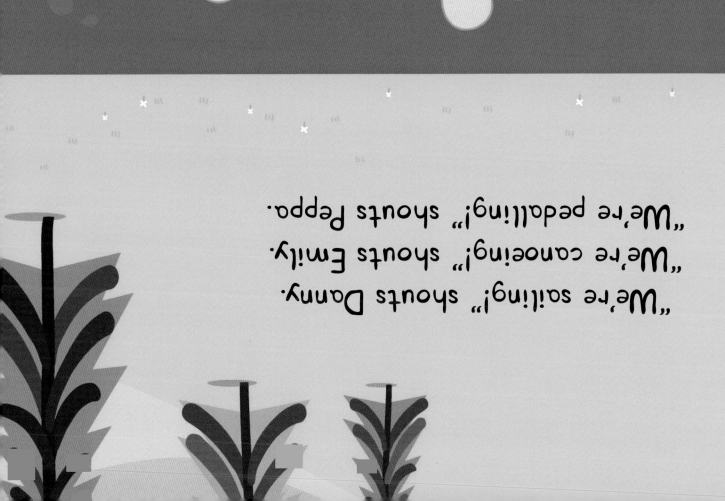

"We're sailing!" shouts Danny.
"We're canoeing!" shouts Emily.
"We're pedalling!" shouts Peppa.

"Aye, aye, Captain, I mean, Dad!" says Danny Dog.

"Ahoy there, Miss Rabbit!
It's Danny Dog and his dad, Captain Dog!
They want to go out in a sailing boat.

"Certainly!" says Miss Rabbit.

Emily Elephant
and her family arrive.
"Hello Miss Rabbit,"
says Mr Elephant. "We'd
like a canoe please!"

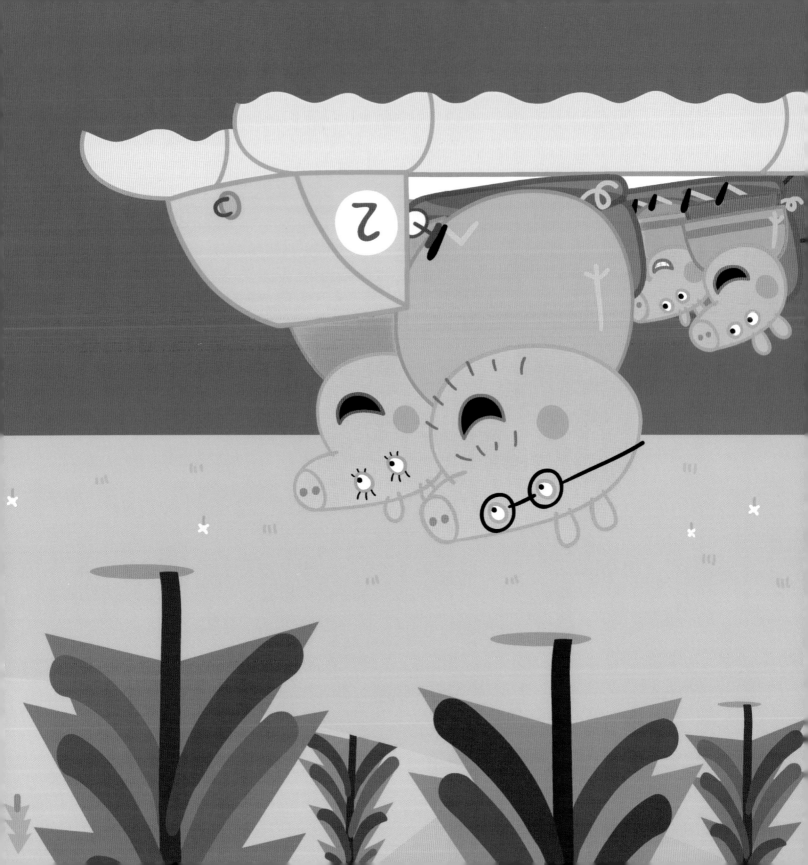

Splish! Splosh!

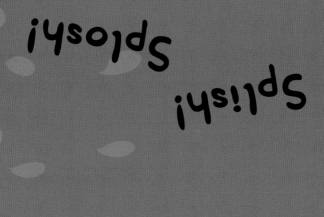

Daddy Pig, Mummy Pig, Peppa and George all climb onto a pedalo. "You have to pedal," Miss Rabbit tells them. "Enjoy your boat trip!" "Off we go!" shouts Daddy Pig. Peppa and George giggle. It's like a bicycle on the water!

"The pedalos look nice and relaxing," smiles Mummy Pig. "Yes!" agrees Daddy Pig. "They've got a big paddle wheel to make them go."

"I've got sailing boats,"
says Miss Rabbit.
Daddy Pig isn't sure.
Sailing a sailing boat is
a bit tricky.

"I've got canoes,"
says Miss Rabbit.
"Hmm . . ." says Daddy Pig.
"Paddling a canoe
is hard work."

"Boats! Boats! Get your boats here!"
calls Miss Rabbit.

Peppa and her family have come to the
lake to go boating.

Peppa Goes Boating

This book is based on the
TV series *Peppa Pig*
Peppa Pig is created by
Neville Astley and Mark Baker

Peppa Pig © Astley Baker Davies Ltd/
Entertainment One UK Ltd 2003
www.peppapig.com

Ladybird

Ladybird Books
Published by the Penguin Group. London, New York, Australia,
Canada, India, Ireland, New Zealand and South Africa
Penguin Books Ltd, Registered Offices: 80 Strand, London WC2R 0RL, England
ladybird.com
First published 2014
002
Adapted by Mandy Archer